HAZE

HAZE

....

E. KRUGER

A NOVELETTE

CruGuru

HAZE

Copyright © 2013 by CruGuru

ISBN: 978-1-920414-81-8

Published by CruGuru in 2013

www.cruguru.com

Johannesburg, South Africa

HAZE

My therapist looked at me skeptically. She picked up a small leather-bound book and read from it: "It's 1AM on New Year's Day, and so far this year I have had half a cup of coffee, watched forty five minutes worth of infomercials, and tried to jump from my balcony. Twice." She paused before looking up at me. "Is this really all you were able to write in the diary I gave you?" she asked me.

"It was the only interesting thing that happened to me," I answered.

"In three weeks?" She raised a quizzical eyebrow at me.

"Well," I hesitated before going on, "yes."

The therapist sighed dejectedly. This was only our second meeting, and already I had been making life very hard for her.

"Tell me about your life up until now. Pretend this is the first time we've ever met, and I know nothing about you."

"But you do know everything about me. I have a file, don't I?"

"You do. But I want to hear it from you," she persisted.

I took a breath, bracing myself for the task at hand. Speaking about my past wasn't something I particularly enjoyed doing.

My name is Brigand Haze. I was on the brink of death, and this is my story.

*****

Picture a girl riding on a bicycle through a picturesque street in a picturesque suburb. The wind fluffs up her hair and billows her shirt. She passes a series of typically suburban homes, encircled by the oh-so-cliché white picket fences that solemnly guard the plethoras of Technicolor flowers in the gardens of jaded house-wives. One would expect this girl to turn her bike into one of these abundant Edens at any moment. But she doesn't. Instead, she rides forth, to a part of the street where the foliage mysteriously disappears, and the sunlight almost seems to be a little bit dim-mer. There she lays her bicycle to rest on the dead grass in front of an ancient, neglected house, the stuff of horror novels and pest control advertisements. The front door creaks as she pushes it open, just as one would expect it to. The house is dark. The floorboards groan beneath the young girl's feet as she progresses carefully inside. She knows that there is zero probability of anyone being home, yet she calls out. The only answer she receives is the squeaking of the door and the floorboards, and the little flame of hope in her heart flickers and dies. She flops down on a forlorn couch. Her melancholy sigh interrupts the symphony of squeaks from the old house. This girl was me on a very significant day in my existence. I made a decision that day that would have an everlasting effect on my life. Or what was left of it at that stage. Rewind back to the forlorn girl sitting on a forlorn couch, contem-plating her future in judgmental suburbia. Suddenly she jumps up, knowing she is alone in this house and this life, and plods purposefully up the stairs. She violently jerks open a grimy medicine cabinet. Medication containers of all shapes and sizes quiver against each other, as if they can sense what's coming next. The girl gathers the majority of them in her hands and strides into a dark bedroom. She spreads out her newfound collection of remedies on the neatly made bed - in sharp contrast with the rest of the chaotic room. Surveying them carefully, she shoves each into a backpack, along with clothing and food rations consisting of candy bars that had been hidden in her closet. She gathers the little money she has, and makes her way to the musty kitchen. She takes a crumpled piece of paper, and scrawls one final loathing message to her ever-absent mother:

Goodbye.

Her bicycle's wheels rattle sorrowfully as she takes off.

*****

Fast-forward to me, sitting in a rotten little apartment, as I tried to make a living serving questionable people questionable drinks in a questionable bar.

It wasn't hard for me to find a job when I first came to the city. Finding a place to stay with the little money I had was the real challenge. During my first few weeks in the city, my boss and his wife let me sleep on their couch. I was embarrassed to have to leech off of people I hardly knew, but beggars can't be choosers, and my options were much too limited for me to be picky. I was relieved when I finally found a place that I could afford. Somewhere to call home, even if the place was probably a health risk.

My only escape, my only happiness, my sole past time, was staring at the assortment of pills I stole from my mother on my last day in the suburbs. For years I had fought the urge to take one, maybe two, perhaps even three of them, just to see if they would make me feel any better about my failure of a life. But I never did. I merely stared at them and wondered what taking them would be like. Secretly I hoped they would turn to dust in their bottles, so I would never have to find out.

One night, at my less-than-glamorous job, my life would undergo yet another drastic change. This time, for the better. It started the very second I stepped through the door. My boss, who was not the cheeriest person to begin with, greeted me simply by saying: "I hope you have some kind of special secret talent." All I could do was stare at him in awe.

"My singer didn't show up. Either you get on that stage and entertain my customers, or you can find yourself another job." That I could not afford.

I had never had to do anything in front of an audience before, and as I stood upon the stage, an icy fear gripped me. What would I do? Tell a joke? Never. Recite a poem? Over my dead body. The crowd was becoming impatient, and my boss even more so. In a moment of sheer panic and desperation, I belted out the one song my mother would play repeatedly whenever she felt depressed (which was nearly always). As a result of this, it was one of the only songs I knew by heart, and it would be the song that changed my life forever. Shifting uncomfortably on the bar stool that had been placed on the pseudo-stage for me, I began:

Love is a burning thing
And it makes a fiery ring...

I paused. A thumbs up and a very rare smile from my boss encouraged me to go on. It turned out I did have a special secret talent – so secret that I didn't even know about it myself.

A few nights after my shaky accidental debut, I was in the back of a shiny Rolls Royce discussing recording contracts and drinking champagne with a man named Arbie Petty, my soon-to-be manager and close friend. Before that day, I had never felt special or unique. But as the crowd cheered for me on that first night, and the nights that followed, I felt as if I had something to offer the world.

*****

Skip ahead a few months to the week after fame hit me in the face like a rogue wave. In just a few short months my new unintentional career had brought me much success. My popularity among the public was skyrocketing faster than I could handle. I couldn't go outside without seeing blown-up versions of my own face on walls and billboards and even a few buses. I couldn't stay inside my luxurious new house without hearing my own voice on the radio at least once a day. Arbie had been good to me. Fame, however, had not.

It was fifteen minutes before my first big concert. When Arbie told me how many people I would be performing for, I wanted to faint. This would be nothing like singing for a few people at the bar – and even that scared me. How would I deal with this? Anxiety and adrenalin pumped rapidly through my veins and ate away at them like acid. On my dresser, among the various perfumes and lipsticks, stood a bottle of putrid pink anti-anxiety pills. Arbie had left them there, instructing me to take one, but only if I felt 'too overwhelmed.' They beckoned me to try them, guaranteeing that my nervousness would disappear instantly. But I couldn't.

And yet, I did. I popped open the cap and opened my shaking palm welcomingly as they slid into my hand. I looked at the label warning me against over-dosage and laughed. In the background, I could hear the near-deafening the roar of the crowd. I slipped the tiny pills into my mouth individually and counted them as I did so:

One.
Ladies and gentlemen.
Two.
Put your hands together.
Three.
For the one.

Four.
The only.
Five.
Miss Brigand Haze.

Show time.

The next thing I remember was walking through a dark corridor back to the dressing room whilst receiving pats on the back from people I had never seen before and would probably never see again. I remember sitting down on a sickeningly green couch. Then everything went black.

*****

A bright fluorescent hospital light and a monotonous beeping lulled me back into consciousness. Arbie, looking as if he'd been sitting at my bedside for several eternities, slowly raised his head upon noticing that I was awake.

"How long have I been here?" I croaked.

"Three days," he answered absently.

"How long have you been here?"

"Three days."

"Sorry," I murmured.

Then it was as if every one of his previously dormant emotions erupted all at once.

"Sorry?" he exploded. "I've been sitting here for three days, expecting the absolute worst, beside myself with worry, and you're sorry?"

I was too dumbstruck to answer.

"The doctor says you're lucky to be alive!" he bellowed on. "We were expecting you to have brain damage or to be permanently comatose." He took a deep breath and carried on. "What would I have done if you died?" he asked.

I shrugged. "Written me a touching eulogy?"

"I'm serious, Brig," he sighed.

"How about a witty epitaph?" I answered, playfully.

"I'm serious!" he roared.

Even though I had only known Arbie for a few months, I knew that he was an all-round sensitive man. I had never seen him this furious before. His anger shocked me into silence.

"Did you do this on purpose?" he asked softly.

"No." It seemed I had suddenly gone hoarse.

"I'm going to ask you again. And I don't want you to lie to me," he breathed. "Did you do this on purpose?"

"No," I answered again, louder this time.

The look in Arbie's eyes gave me a clear indication that he didn't believe me, but the smile on his face said otherwise.

"Then let's get you out of here, shall we?"

*****

Two weeks after my 'unfortunate collapse' (as the papers so diplomatically called Arbie's sugar-coated story stating that I was simply 'stressed'), I was back to normal. Whatever that was. One too bright morning, the shrill ringing of the phone pierced through my already flimsy skull. It was Arbie, announcing that I would be appearing on some ostentatious talk show that evening. My only reply was a dejected groan. It would be my first real interview, and I was not excited. Later that day, whilst brushing my teeth and cursing the day I was born, I calculated whether a jump from my balcony would be fatal. This was something I seemed to be doing all too often. Checking my watch, I decided that it would have to wait until after my television appearance.

Upon arriving at the studio, I was instructed to wait my turn in a cramped and badly decorated excuse of a waiting room. After a few minutes of agonizing solitude in my *feng shui* prison, I was joined by a fairly tall, thin man with wavy auburn hair and the most exquisite pair of hands I had ever seen. He introduced himself as Rip Laurent. The introduction wasn't necessary, however, as he was, like myself, a rather famous singer, and very unlike myself, a brilliant singer at that.

"What brings a talented artist like you to a horrific studio like this?" he asked in a desperate attempt to break the ice.

"My manager," I snorted.

"Where are you from?" he enquired. Normally my bluntness scared people off immediately, but this man was not going down without a fight.

"Far away." Another snort on my part.

"You aren't really one for making conversation, are you?" he tried.

"Let's just say it isn't exactly my forte."

Mercifully, a crewmember came to my rescue and whisked me away to the make-up room.

"By the way, Mr. Laurent," I said as I left the room, "you have a milk moustache."

I left him wiping fervently at the non-existent stain on his face.

Bright lights and forced applause welcomed me as I walked onto the set after the show's pompous host announced my arrival a little too loudly. At first, we talked about my career, discussed my humble beginnings, made a few jokes, and the norm. Then, the inevitable: "Tell us a bit about your little fainting spell a couple of weeks ago. What happened?" the host asked. I prepared myself to recite the cover story that Arbie and I had been practising since I left the hospital.

"I was just under a lot of stress. The tension got too much, I suppose," I said.

"Is there anything else, in your opinion, which could have triggered it?" the host asked again. It appeared I had a nosy parker on my hands.

"Like I said, I was under a lot of pressure. I was probably just nervous about my first big performance. That's all," I answered in such an impolite manner that I might as well have been saying, "Let it go, you blithering imbecile."

Lucky for both of us, he got the message and changed the subject. "Brigand," he began, "That's a very interesting name. Won't you tell us where it comes from?" In my mind, I laughed in the pompous host's face.

Brigand. Noun. Robber, bandit, outlaw.

What was I supposed to say?

I took a deep breath before answering. "My mother simply liked the sound of the word. She didn't bother looking up its meaning until I was about thirteen, and by then it was too late to do anything about it."

After a brief silence, Pompous Host began to laugh, thinking I had made a joke. The audience was soon to follow. Little did they know I was telling the truth. So I laughed along and left it at that.

After my complete failure of an interview, followed by Rip's rather riveting one, Pompous Host asked me to sing a song, which I did, once again with the help of my pharmaceutical friends. I was still intimidated by the crowd in front of me, even if it was considerably smaller than the one at my first concert. When my little tune was over, it was the turn of the great Rip Laurent to entertain the audience. From the first note to the last, I was captivated. A few times, I caught myself gaping at him with my mouth wide open. I attributed this enchantment to the fact that I was slightly Under the Influence. After the dreadful show had finally ended, I rushed to gather my things in order to leave as soon as possible. I was startled by Rip's velvet voice speaking suddenly behind me.

"You lied to me."

"What?" I asked, baffled.

"In the waiting room, you said I had a milk moustache. But my face was clean, wasn't it? You lied."

"I was bored," I said, shrugging my shoulders, attempting to escape yet again.

"Any good singer knows it's a bad idea to have dairy before performing."

"You were worried about it anyway, weren't you?" I really wished he would leave, and take his perfect voice and beautiful hands with him.

"If you must know, I did have a bit of a drink before coming here. I thought maybe traces of it were still on my face," he said.

"Bit of a drinker, are we?" I chuckled.

"Well, I...I," he stammered.

"I'm joking," I smiled, and began to walk toward the exit of the building.

"Come to think of it," he said, following me outside, "I think I'd like to have another. With you."

Once again, I didn't know what to say. This appeared to be happening to me much too often to my liking.

"Well?" he asked after a long pause.

I contemplated his offer a while longer.

And accepted.

A few hours and a number of drinks later, Rip and I found ourselves atop the roof of an apartment building, singing incoherent songs at the top of our voices. After a moment's silence, Rip stood closer to the edge of the roof, beginning to whistle as he did so.

"I wish I could shout all my innermost thoughts from up here," he said.

"So, why don't you?"

"Don't have the guts," he sighed.

In response to this, I joined him at the roof's edge and yelled as loud as I could:

"I am young, I am angry, I am drunk, and nobody understands me!"

A few passers-by below stopped to applaud me, and I responded with a courteous curtsy.

Upon returning home in the early morning hours, I decided not to leap from my balcony after all.

*****

Time passed by, slowly but surely. Weeks became months, months became years. Performing came to be more than simply my job, but my life. I had been able to go on stage without the help of medication. The crowds became less daunting. My heart didn't beat as rapidly before stepping on stage. I somehow coaxed myself into calmness, most nights.

I had also made a friend in Rip, who called every week and visited as often as his schedule allowed. Things were looking up. Or so I thought.

During my years as a performer, I had contracted a number of diva-esque mannerisms, which I rather enjoyed using in attempts to drive my dear friend Arbie insane. One morning, when I was feeling particularly impossible, Arbie came to see me. It was far past noon, and I was still curled up in bed, with no intention of getting up. Arbie seemed frazzled at this, and rightly so, as I had a very important concert that evening, incidentally at the same venue where I had had my 'collapse' just a few years before. This was one of the main reasons for my unwillingness to drag myself out of bed. Arbie was trying exceedingly hard to convince me to leave my linen haven.

"Brig, please, get out of bed. I'm begging you. Get up. Get ready. Entertain your adoring public. Please," he pleaded.

I opened my eyes, raised an uninterested eyebrow at him, and closed them again.

"Brigand!" he cried. "Come on, sweetheart. We'll make tonight's concert special, eh? What do you say? A big show. I'll get you anything you want."

"Anything?" I asked, suddenly giving him my undivided attention.

"Just say the word," he answered with a silly grin.

"I want a bubble canon," I said in a blasé tone.

"Brig, honey, I'll get you fifty bubble canons if you'll just get up!" Arbie exclaimed.

"For fifty bubble canons, I'll get up twice," I said as I hopped out of bed with newfound enthusiasm.

"I will never understand you," Arbie laughed as he left the room in order for me to dress.

That evening as I stood in front of the mirror in the musty dressing room, readying myself for the performance to come, the same icy fear that had gripped me before that first concert took hold of my insides once more. The smell of the dressing room took me back to that first night. I heard the people cheering. I thought about how many of them were out there. And it scared me. For the first time in years, it scared me. There were pills in the top drawer of the dresser. I knew there were. I was the one who put them there. Just in case. But I couldn't do it. I couldn't take them. Not this time. Not again.

Half an hour before show time. The pills had now made their way to the top of the dresser. My insides were yelling, screaming, aching for me to grab them and swallow them one by one. But my brain was telling me to stop. To consider the consequences. To remember what happened last time. To learn from my past mistakes. To walk away.

I took a deep breath and fled the room.

The venue's swinging back doors flapped shut behind me as I stood outside, breathing in the frosty evening air.

Veni. I came.

Vidi. I saw.

Running back into the building, tears began to stream down my face. I was too afraid. I had to do it. I grabbed the pills and swallowed a bunch at once.

I did not conquer.

Another deep breath, and the blinding stage lights welcomed me once more. The music began. And I allowed the medication to do its job while I did mine.

Another hazy performance, another blackout, another brush with death, another beeping EKG machine ushering me back into the land of the living. All that was different this time around was that I now had not one, but two concerned watchers at my bedside, in the form of Arbie and Rip.

Arbie took a breath, as if preparing to deliver a berating speech.

"Save it," I coughed.

"No," he began, "I will not 'save it', Brigand. I thought we were through with this. I thought that after your first time in the hospital you would have stopped with this madness of yours."

"Looks like you thought wrong," I remarked, scornfully.

At this, Arbie glared hatefully at me and stormed out of the room. He went through a lot of trouble to slam the door behind him, conveying the already clear message that he was beside himself with anger.

I jumped as Rip began to speak. I had nearly forgotten that he was in the room.

"So," he sighed, "it isn't the first time something like this has happened to you?"

"No," I answered with a roll of my eyes.

"I'm coming to stay with you for a while. Arbie asked me to. And I want to."

"I don't need a guard dog."

"Have you ever considered, you know, getting help?" he asked, hesitantly.

"Excuse me?"

"Look at yourself," he went on, vexed, "Look at where you are. You need someone to look after you. You're unstable; you obviously can't be left alone --"

"Unstable?" I interrupted him. "How dare you?" I cried, sitting upright.

"It's the truth!" he screamed.

"Get out," I breathed, my voice shaking with fury.

He did not move, but stood firmly rooted to his spot in front of my hospital bed.

"I said, get out!" I screeched.

At first, it seemed as if Rip was considering defying my request once more. However, he gave up and exited the room in high dudgeon, leaving me to struggle with my regret in solitude.

*****

One chaotic week later, I was home. Rip, unfortunately, was with me. Throughout my stay at the hospital, I had gotten into several fights with several psychologists. They all offered their so-called help, but I was convinced that I didn't need it.

By order of Arbie, Rip was to accompany me home and stay there with me until he was absolutely, positively convinced that it was safe to leave me on my own again. Concerts, interviews and photo shoots that had been scheduled for the coming weeks were all postponed. The rags that called themselves newspapers all reported the same story: I had had another regrettable fainting spell after a show. Some of them even went as far as expressing their concern for my health and general well-being. Hypocrites.

To my great disliking, Rip made himself comfortable on my pricey couch as if it were his own. Had it been anybody else, I wouldn't have minded in the least, but the problem was that I had developed a certain fondness for Rip which both frightened and somewhat engrossed me.

Of course, I could never profess this fondness to anyone. Let alone myself.

Hence my uneasiness with his living in my home.

The days dragged by all too slowly, and I was becoming rather annoyed with being cooped up like an inmate in my own house. As a result of my annoyance, Rip and I fought almost daily, if not hourly.

"I want to go out," I declared one bright, sundrenched morning.

"You're sick," Rip answered, sprawled on the couch with a magazine resting lazily upon his face.

"I feel better, Rip. I want to leave the house. Just for a little while," I begged.

"No," he grunted from his indolent position on the sofa.

I rose purposefully from the chair I was sitting in. "I'm leaving," I said, firmly. "And you can't stop me."

"The hell I can't," he growled as he jumped up from the couch and grabbed me forcefully by the wrists.

"I can't stay in here anymore. It's been two weeks, I need to be outside! Let me go outside," I pleaded, all whilst struggling against Rip's powerful grip.

"You're right, Brig, it's been two weeks. Only two weeks. Do you really want people to see you like this?" he said softly, still pinning my arms down.

"Are you saying I look like some junkie?" I asked, offended.

"That's exactly what I'm saying," he barked, gradually releasing me from his grasp.

Tears spilled from my eyes. "Is that what you think of me?" I whimpered.

"No. And it's not what I want other people to think of you. Which is why you need to stay inside. Just for a little while long-er."

I retreated toward the couch and wept even more.

"Please, don't cry," Rip whispered, sitting down next to me, reluctantly.

As if bound by some order, some command, I stopped crying nearly immediately.

"Arbie is coming over tonight to check on you," Rip said as he rose from his seat and departed from the room.

When Arbie arrived, I did my best to stay out of his way, as we had not exactly spoken since our disagreement at the hospital a few weeks before. Hiding out in the room adjacent to my living room, I could hear him speaking to Rip. Driven by curiosity, I leaned against the door and listened in on their muffled conversation.

"How is she?" Arbie enquired. Cliché, cliché, cliché.

"She feels trapped inside the house," Rip answered, seemingly emotionless.

"She can't go out, Rip. Not while she's like this. She's not well. You have to understand." Arbie's tone sped up a bit as he said this.

He was making it sound as if I were a psychopath.

"She can't stay locked up in her own home, either. She needs to go outside, take a walk. Breathe in the fresh air, feel the sun on her face, see the clouds, hear the birds," Rip argued.

Arbie gave in almost too easily.

"Very well. Take her out tomorrow, then. But only for a short while, and only if you're entirely certain that she'll be okay. I'm trusting you with her." Again he was making it seem as if I were some fragile little thing that would shatter at the slightest exposure to any sort of adversity.

"She'll be fine, Arbie. I promise," Rip assured him in a near-whisper. "She's been feeling a lot better."

"And you?" Arbie asked. "How have you been feeling?"

"Oh," Rip sighed, "you know."

"No. Actually I don't."

Another miserable sigh from Rip. "I love her and she hates everyone."

A gasp lost its way somewhere between my throat and my lips. I felt as though all my airways had been sealed off. I steadied myself against the door, struggling to breathe.

Rip? Love? Me?

Madness.

Folly.

Lunacy.

It simply wasn't possible.

In my daze, I hadn't heard that Arbie had left and that Rip was now calling to me.

Still overcome with shock and astonishment, I ran to my bedroom and hopped into bed, pretending to be sound asleep.

"Brig?" I heard Rip say as my bedroom door creaked open. I heard him come in, and felt him sit down at the foot of the bed. I was completely still, doing my best not to make any sound or movement. I don't know how long he sat there. All I know is that the entire time, I had to fight against the urge to sit up and tell him what I had heard. But he couldn't know. Not ever.

The next morning, Rip woke me up while it was still dark. "What's going on?" I asked, confused and groggy.

"We're going out. Just like you asked." He smiled faintly.

"Now?"

"Now."

I was still half asleep when I collapsed into the passenger's seat of Rip's car.

"Where are we going?"

"Far away," he answered with yet another slight smile.

"Seriously."

"Do you remember when we first met? I asked you where you were from. You said 'far away'. So that's where we're going."

"Are you really that desperate to see the place I'm from?" I couldn't help but laugh.

"Yes, I am. Unless there's somewhere else you'd rather go."

Every ounce of my logic commanded me, begged me to say, "Yes, Rip, I'd rather go someplace else. I'm not ready to go home. Not yet."

But instead, after a moment's hesitation, I said, "Fine. We can visit my old home. But you're not going to like it."

I knew I had made a terrible mistake the second Rip started his car.

*****

The anchor that was chained to my heart became heavier and heavier as we neared the good old 'burbs where I had spent the majority of my lonely childhood. I considered jumping from the car at every red light and every stop sign. We came closer and closer to my former address, until, eventually, we grinded to a halt in front of the barren yard and broken-down house that I unenthusiastically called home so many years before. I wondered if my mother was home. Or if she even still lived there. I hoped for neither.

"This is where you used to live?" Rip asked in disbelief.

"I told you, you wouldn't like it," I answered, blandly.

"Brigand, if I'd known you had it this bad..." His voice trailed off.

"Now do you see why I didn't want to tell you where I came from when we first met?"

"Yes," he choked out.

Rip opened his car door, readying himself to get out.

"What are you doing?" I was alarmed at his action.

"You want to go in, don't you?"

"Wait," I said, pulling him lightly back into the car. He sat back down and shut his door.

"There's something I need to tell you, if we're going to go inside," I continued.

Rip didn't reply.

"I ran away from here. When I'd just finished school."

"What?" he breathed.

"I'm not even sure if my mother still lives here. I haven't seen her in years." My voice was trembling now.

"And your father?" Rip asked.

"Never knew him."

"Why'd you run away?"

"Take a look inside the house, and you'll understand why," I said as I opened my door, left the car and marched across the street towards the old place.

I pressed the doorbell and jumped when it rang, amazed that the thing still worked.

Rip had caught up to me in the meantime and was now standing behind me. His presence was comforting.

I pressed the doorbell again. No response. Why did I expect anything different?

I pushed the door. It was unlocked and screeched open easily. Nothing new there, either.

I stepped inside, the floorboards creaking below me as I did so. Just like old times.

"Nobody's home," Rip said, hesitantly. "Do you think she still lives here?" he asked me.

"She definitely does," I said, looking at the empty medication containers and bottles that had been strewn across the filthy living room. Rip stood motionless, staring at them too. He didn't say anything, but it was easy enough to guess what he was thinking. He was most likely thinking that my mother must have been a terrible person. And that she probably still is. He was thinking that he could understand where my love for all things medicinal came from. That the apple didn't fall far from the tree. I couldn't blame him for thinking that. He was right, after all.

"You know," I sighed, sinking down onto the faded and aged couch, "After I'd left, she didn't even come looking for me. She never tried to find me, as far as I know. It was as if she hadn't even noticed I was gone."

"If you hadn't left here, things would have been a lot different for you."

"If I'd never left this place, I'd probably still be stuck here, financing my mother's habits, because she's too pathetic to care for her sorry self." I felt embarrassed about my little outburst, but did my best not to show it.

"You had no choice," Rip said, softly, sitting down next to me.

I sensed a flood of tears coming on, but prevented them just in time. I rose from the couch and made my way to my old bedroom, leaving Rip by himself in the living room. Other than being dustier than before, it was exactly as I had left it. I sat down on my old bed, breathing in the familiar smells of home I so despised when I was younger. I closed my eyes for a moment, losing myself in my surroundings, allowing the memories to come flooding back. I remembered a fight I'd had with my mother a few days before I left, in that very room. It was as if sitting in my former bedroom allowed me to see an instant replay of that day. It was something I'd rather not have thought about, but I couldn't help myself. The memory seemed to be pushing its way through my subconscious, until the events came alive before my eyes.

There she stood, my dear absentee mother, in all her faux glory.

"If you hate me so much, how come you haven't left yet?" I remember her asking me, her voice raspy from all the cancer sticks she smoked each day.

I stood up with rare confidence. I was determined to face her that day. To let her know what she was doing to me.

"I haven't left because I care," I replied. My tone was aggressive, and I liked it that way.

"You filthy little liar," she sniggered, "You haven't left yet because you have nowhere else to go. You couldn't care less about me. But that's all right."

"If that's what you think, then maybe I really should leave," I spat.

"If you go out that door, you are dead to me," she snarled. "I hope you understand that."

Infuriated, I gathered my belongings and attempted to leave my room and head for the front door. My mother barred the way. I pushed against her, to no avail. She had always been much stronger than I was. In one swift movement, she had shoved me to the floor and grabbed me by the hair. I cried out, even though I knew very well that no one could hear me.

I forced my thoughts back into the present. I didn't want to remember anything further than that.

"Brigand?"

I had become so wrapped up in my memories that I hadn't even heard Rip calling me. I didn't want to face him in the state I was in. I plodded down the stairs. The living room was empty. I figured he must have gone upstairs in search of me. I seized the opportunity and ran out the front door, leaving him alone inside the old house. I ran towards a place where I remembered there being an open field, where I would be surrounded by grass much taller than myself. It was a place I had retreated to many times before. I could be at peace there.

Upon arriving at the field, I collapsed in the shelter of the tall grass, and sobbed.

I detested her.

She detested me.

Her words kept repeating in my head, over and over and over again.

"You are dead to me."

I had to make myself believe that I never cared. That it never bothered me.

I didn't care then, and I don't care now.

I didn't care then.

I don't care now.

I don't care.

I don't care.

I don't care.

I cried myself to sleep in that open field. The moaning wind was my blanket, and the sorrowful birdsong my lullaby.

I awoke to the sound of my name being called in a familiar voice. Two familiar voices.

"Brigand!" Rip.

"Brigand!" Arbie.

Involuntarily, I found myself eavesdropping on another one of their conversations.

"I trusted you with her, Rip! How do you lose an adult human being?" Arbie roared.

"She knows this place better than I do. I've never been here before. How was I supposed to know where she was going?" Rip said, flustered.

"Did you even try to follow her?" Arbie seemed exceedingly irritated.

"I did. Really, I did. But she was out of the house before I even realized she was missing. I'm sure she'll come back. I'm sure." It sounded as though he was trying to convince himself more than he was trying to convince Arbie.

"I hope you're right." I heard Arbie sigh. "This is my fault. I knew she wasn't ready to leave the house yet." It sounded like he might have been crying.

"No," said Rip, "it's my fault. I should've known better than to bring her here. I'm the one who suggested we come and see her old home, without even knowing the circumstances of her child-hood. I should've known something bad happened to her here, since she never wanted to talk about the place. She was ready to go out of the house. She just wasn't ready to come back here. She wasn't ready to confront her past."

It sounded like Rip was in tears, too.

Suddenly, I heard the sound of feet crushing the grass. Arbie and Rip were nearing me, both still sniffing somewhat. I curled up and acted as if I were asleep.

Arbie found me first.

"Brigand?" he whispered. I opened my eyes and sat upright.

"Hi," I mumbled, rubbing my eyes.

"Don't you ever scare me like that again!" Arbie yelled, grab-bing me.

I thought he might have another lecture in store for me, but instead he simply held me like he would a little girl. A daughter.

"Let's go home," Rip said, placing his hand on my shoulder.

Our walk back to the car was silent; the drive home even more so.

It was after this that my lifestyle and my state of mind took a turn for the absolute worst.

*****

Move ahead a few months to Rip and I attending the most atro-cious party in history. I never liked social gatherings to begin with, but that night I felt particularly unenthusiastic. Unenthusiastic enough to eat my weight in party snacks and die of food poisoning right in front of the lackluster host and all his unexciting guests. Rip was lost somewhere in the ocean of people swaying to the beat of the most abysmal music I had ever been forced to listen to. I was, as had always been my habit at such events, sitting at the makeshift bar on an unsteady chair, consuming a deadly mixture of alcohol and complimentary peanuts. From somewhere in between the crowds of dancing people and the clusters of voices trying to converse above the din of the music, Rip emerged and seated himself on the vacant chair next to mine. We stared blankly at each other for a while, until Rip's eyes began to drift lazily about the room, searching for nothing in particular. Socially, we were not having the most productive evening.

In the short silence between the end of one song and the start of the next, a young woman entered the room. Quite a few people took notice of her, but as the next song began, they soon forgot about her and continued with whatever it was they were doing before. I was surprised to see that she was making her way towards Rip and I. As she came closer, Rip rose from his seat and called to her.

"Isabella!"

"Ripley!"

I sat, frozen, watching the scene play out before me. The woman greeted me with great zeal, but I remained in my chair and merely gave her an absent wave.

In short, Isabella was a concert pianist who had just returned from living in Spain for five years. She and Rip had known each other since their schooldays. She was tall, tanned and slim, and I hated her. I didn't hate her because she was mean or because she was a bad person. She was the exact opposite. She was perfect. She was nice, she was courteous, she was gorgeous – and I loathed her for it. I hated the lovely, clear laugh that spilled from her faultless cherry lips; I hated her flowing jet-black hair, I hated her intense hazel eyes, and I hated her delicate tan hands which swept surreptitiously across Rip's forearm every so often. Every time she giggled at something he said, or vice versa, I wished someone would assassinate me through the nearest window, or poison my martini while I wasn't looking. Regrettably, neither of these happened. And yet, somewhere amid the introductions and mechanical small talk, I managed to smile and be adequately friendly. This friendliness was short-lived, however. After about half an hour of pretending to listen to Rip and Isabella's mindless chatter, I had become rather fed up with their ignoring my existence. Rip asking Isabella to dance was the last straw. As they made their way to the crammed dance floor, I gathered my things, telephoned my driver, and made my way home. I didn't know if they would even notice that I had left, and I didn't really care much either.

After an agonizing drive, the car finally came to a standstill in front of my house. I thanked the driver and made my way up the front steps. As I closed the front door behind me, I leaned with my back against it and began to sob.

*****

I tried to be nice to Isabella. I really did. After all, she had done nothing to make me dislike her. In fact, she had been nothing but kind to me ever since the night we met. I vowed to maintain a benevolent attitude toward her, or to at least attempt to. Somehow I had to mask the real reason for my aversion of her – pure and untainted jealousy. When I first realized that I was, in fact, envious of Isabella and that my envy had been the cause of my weeping spell the night of the party, I felt embarrassed and ridiculous. How could I allow something so trivial to upset me this way? I had to shake it off – if Rip someday found happiness with her, who was I to be discontented and miserable about it? Who was I to stand in their way? As if I could offer him anything better. As if I could ever measure up to her perfection, the flawless precision with which she conducted every aspect of her life.

I decided to put whatever fondness I may have still fostered for Rip behind me. I would be the better person. I would grant him his happiness. I would be selfless, altruistic. A complete contradiction of my true self. Within the week, Rip unknowingly presented me with the perfect opportunity to put my new philanthropic outlook on life into practice.

Arbie, Isabella and I had all gathered at Rip's private studio to listen to a new song which he claimed he had been working on for months and was finally ready to present to ears other than his own and those of his instrumentalists. As we listened, I incessantly pinched the soft skin on the back of my hand, in order to forget about my feelings of jealousy toward Isabella. I kept repeating to myself that she was a refined, gracious person who meant me no harm. I had no reason to dislike or distrust her. Despite my efforts, I found it increasingly difficult not to flee the room in a huff of pathetic tears.

As Rip's song came to an end and we all complimented him in turn, I noticed the woman behind the drum set gazing intently at me. Her hair was a dark brown tangle of colorfully beaded braids. She was barefoot, and wore a flowing indigo dress and round John Lennon glasses – the kind with the bluish tint to their lenses. Wanting to be as far from Isabella and her sweet laugh as I possibly could, I decided to approach her. Before I could even introduce myself, the woman spoke. "You don't like her, do you?"

She had caught me off guard. "Don't like who?" I stuttered.

"The pretty girl with the black hair."

I groaned. "Is it that obvious?"

She gave me a shrewd smile. "Not to anyone else, no. But to me it is." She offered me her hand. "I'm Julienne, by the way. Julienne Tracy." I shook her hand politely. "And I'm--"

"Brigand Haze, right?" she cut me short. "The whole world knows who you are," she smirked.

Rip chose that moment to join us. "Brig," he beamed, "I see you've met my new drummer."

I nodded.

He grinned at Julienne as he put his hand possessively around my shoulder and said, "Perhaps one day you could play for Brigand. She's spectacular." He pinched my cheek and returned to Arbie and Isabella. I could feel my face contort into a lamentable expression. Goodbye new, unselfish life. So much for putting my feelings for Rip behind me.

From behind the drums, Julienne shook her head. "Brigand Haze," she sighed, "you look like you need a drink."

A few minutes later, I found myself following Julienne into a place called Sue's, and within seconds of entering the room, we were both seated and holding drinks – on the house, the waiter assured us. It appeared that Julienne was a regular there. At first, she and I spoke of everyday things, telling each other about ourselves and such. But as the night progressed I found myself growing more and more at ease in her company. Perhaps it was the alcohol, but I preferred to think that it was due to Julienne's contagious smile and sociable personality. When not behind her beloved drum set, Julienne liked drinking, smoking, and eating junk food - in that order. She adored being the center of attention, and, ironically enough, the only time she ever gave up her place in the spotlight to anyone else was on stage.

"You know, sometimes I think I was born behind a drum kit," she declared later in the evening, after we had both become considerably merry.

"That's my opinion, anyway," she continued. "Not like I'd know where I was born."

This statement confused me. "How so?"

"I was an orphan, Brigand Haze, a stray. It's all very sad really, but look at me now!" she cried, rising from her seat, only to fall right back into it again.

"What about you? Parents? Siblings?" she asked, after regaining her balance.

"I have a mom, I suppose," I responded, hesitantly.

"You suppose?" She seemed puzzled.

I couldn't bring myself to answer her.

"Let me guess, your relationship with her isn't exact-ly...favorable, is it? Did you fight a lot?"

"When she was home," I answered, bluntly.

She nodded understandingly. "Look, I've been in enough foster homes to understand what bad parents are like. I get it." After a short silence she went on, "You know something?"

"What?" I asked, resting my chin in my palm.

"We're kindred spirits, you and I. We should be friends, Brig- and Haze." She took a crude sip of her drink.

"I thought we already were," I said.

"Then it's decided," she grinned, raising her empty glass, letting the melting ice inside it glisten under the bright lamp above our heads.

After that first night out with Julienne, I finally felt as if I had made a true friend. Of course Arbie was my friend, but I couldn't share things with him like I could with Julienne. And of course Rip was my friend as well - my best friend - but he had hurt me deeply. Even if he was oblivious of that fact. After that evening, Julienne and I were inseparable. We spoke every day and made plans to see each other whenever we could. For the first time in my life, I felt that I was not alone.

*****

A few uneventful weeks had passed by almost unnoticed when the shrill ring of the telephone woke me early one balmy morning.

"Hello?" I said groggily into the receiver.

"Brig? I hope you're free tonight." It was Rip.

"I suppose," I answered. A sudden optimism crept into my mind that maybe, just maybe, the two of us would be able to spend the evening together with no one else around to interfere. The idea was absurd, I knew, but I couldn't help hoping.

"I'm throwing a going-away party for Isabella, and I'd like you to be there," he said from the other end of the phone.

My heart sank. Of course. How silly of me. On the bright side, a going-away party meant that Isabella was leaving. Hopefully for good. I scolded myself for thinking something so mean, but couldn't help it.

"Going away?" I asked, trying not to sound too happy. "Where to?"

"Back to Spain." He sounded genuinely disappointed.

"Oh," I replied, "that's too bad." I felt like a chump for not having anything more comforting to say. I took a deep breath. "Of course I'll be there."

After hanging up, I felt listless, yet strangely content. Saying that I had mixed emotions would have been an understatement. I decided to call Julienne immediately and ask her to accompany me. This was one occasion I could not face on my own.

Rip's house had always reminded me of what Jay Gatsby's place would have looked like if it were slightly smaller and more contemporarily furnished, especially when he threw big parties. Entering through his hand-carved front door, I was engulfed by a sort of warmth that always made me feel welcome in his home. But that night I felt uneasy. There was an ominous sort of atmosphere about the evening, and I had a strange feeling that I might not go home happy at the end of the night. I did my best to ignore this premonition though, and instead searched for Julienne in the crowd. If there was anyone who could help me forget my anxiousness, it was her. At last she emerged; drink in hand, wearing the same indigo dress she had worn on the day we met. Her hair, however, was slightly neater this time, piled tidily on top of her head and expertly held together by rainbow-colored pins. Before I had the chance to greet her, Isabella appeared from the kitchen and accompanied us to the living room. She looked beautiful in a striking olive green dress. In her all-too-perfect way, she thanked us both for attending and spoke of how sad she was about having to leave so soon. I didn't really pay attention, and heaved a miserable sigh when she finally left us.

"She's pretty," I remarked, absently.

"Pretty annoying," Julienne snorted.

"She annoys you?" I gasped. I was both shocked and surprised to find that there was someone other than myself who didn't perceive Isabella as the perfect specimen of a human being.

"She is just too flawless. Her personality, her looks, the way she does things – it's all too immaculate. Nobody's that perfect." She crossed her arms, suddenly wound up.

She turned around swiftly and abruptly to hail a waiter. She took two glasses of champagne from his tray and with a motion of her head, she beckoned for me to follow her. "Come on, we need to sit down."

I felt ill at ease for the remainder of the evening. I couldn't help but look up clandestinely every time Isabella walked by. After doing this several times, Julienne inevitably noticed and said, "She annoys you too, doesn't she? The way her hips sway when she walks, the way she has everyone in a trance when she speaks. The way Rip looks at her. It aggravates you, I can tell."

"It doesn't aggravate me, it just--"

"It scares you. You're afraid of losing Rip to this girl. I understand that," she interrupted.

I gave a somber groan in reply.

As the evening dragged on, Julienne and I found ourselves lazing about on Rip's living room couch, completely unfazed by the other guests around us.

"How do you think you'll die?" Julienne asked out of the blue, a cigarette dangling idly from her fingers.

For a brief moment, I considered telling her that I had already brushed with death - twice - and that I no longer cared how my life would end. I decided against it. I would tell her eventually, just not at the party.

"Spontaneous combustion," I responded at last. "You?"

"Knowing myself, I'd probably accidentally walk off a roof in my sleep," she laughed. "Spontaneous combustion, though? That's creative."

She stared intently at her empty champagne glass, until finally she said, "Where have those dear waiters gone?" We scanned the room, but they were nowhere to be seen. "Do you know where the kitchen is in this place?" she asked me.

Wordlessly I stood and signaled for Julienne to follow me as I led the way. Upon reaching the kitchen door, I heard soft voices coming from behind it. Raising my index finger to my lips, motioning for Julienne to be quiet, I slowly pushed open the door. Gazing into the kitchen, I was met by a shattering sight: Isabella and Rip were in each other's arms, entwined in a warm embrace that would most likely remain engraved in my mind for eternity. Instantly realizing my presence, they pulled away from each other, avoided my eyes and seemed humiliated that they had been caught. Not knowing what to say or how to react, I quietly excused myself and fled. They seemed not to notice just how much discovering them had upset me, and I preferred it that way. I had completely forgotten that Julienne was standing behind me and bumped right into her. She had probably seen the whole thing. Avoiding eye-contact, I apologized to her, said goodbye and headed for the front door. On my way, I could distantly hear Julienne speaking to Rip.

"You're an idiot, you know?" I heard her say. At that moment, I felt that she couldn't have been more right, and that her statement applied just as much to me, as well.

*****

After the departure of Isabella, Rip began to call me more often. His visits became more frequent. Now that he no longer had the beautiful Isabella to distract him, it seemed he was more than willing to be my friend once more, as if nothing had ever happened. But, as it would be, when Rip suddenly wanted to see more of me again, I no longer wished to see or speak to him. I couldn't look at his face without agonizing memories of that night piercing into my mind. Ignoring his phone calls and paying no heed to his requests to visit me at home had become my modus operandi. This strategy of ignorance worked well for me, until one night, when the telephone's sharp ring sliced through the darkness of my bedroom.

Fearing the worst, as I always did with late night telephone calls, I answered hesitantly.

"Hello?"

My voice sounded out of place in the shadowy room.

"Brigand? It's Rip." I prepared myself to hang up. "I'm outside. Please come down," he pleaded.

Would I? Would I give in to his request and break my hiatus of not seeing him for weeks? Was I ready to face him, and the recollections of that heartbreaking evening that he brought with him? As much as I wanted to deny it, I really did want to see Rip. I could never admit it to myself or to anyone else, but I did miss him. I missed my friend.

Dragging my feet, I made my way down the stairs and opened the front door. There he stood, shivering in the cold, arms outstretched to greet me, with a ridiculous smile upon his face.

"Why are you here, exactly?" I asked as he stepped inside.

"I wanted to see you," he replied matter-of-factly.

"And this couldn't wait until morning because?" I raised a suspicious eyebrow at him.

"I felt I had to apologize to you," he yawned, habitually making his way over to my couch and seating himself without invitation.

"Apologize? For what?" I crossed my arms, annoyed with his evasiveness.

"I've been neglecting you since Isabella arrived. And I wanted to make amends. I can't go home without your forgiveness, Brigand. Please," he pleaded.

At first, I was angered by his gesture. He woke me up at the most unholy hour of day so that I could be forced to listen to his insincere, dishonest, disingenuous excuse of an apology? And for what? His own peace of mind? Was I the means with which he wished to soothe his guilt for whatever wrongdoing he may have committed?

In my mind I told Rip that I did not accept is apology. I told him to leave. I was brutal and firm. I told him how much he had hurt me and how I did not appreciate his coming to my home and saying sorry to me simply in order to pacify his own feelings of regret. I told him that I did not like to be used. I rejected his false display of remorse.

In reality, the exact opposite happened.

"I'm the one who should be apologizing, Rip."

I mentally berated myself for uttering that phrase the moment I said it.

"And why would that be?" he laughed.

"I was horrible to Isabella, even though she didn't deserve it. I was curt and blunt whenever I spoke to her, although she'd only ever been kind to me. I'm sorry for treating her that way."

With a sigh, I seated myself on the carpet at Rip's feet.

"Shouldn't you be telling her that?" he asked, resting his hand idly on top of my head.

"No," I whispered.

"And why not?"

"I acted that way towards her because of you. I felt that with her in the picture, I'd lose you as a friend, and I didn't want that. That's why."

"You know I would never have let that happen," he said.

We shared a brief, but comfortable silence.

"Are you two still going to carry on seeing each other now that she's gone?" I enquired.

"What do you mean?" he replied, seemingly at a loss.

"Well, after the night of Isabella's farewell party, in the kitchen..." my voice trailed off.

"Oh, no, no!" Rip exclaimed. "We both knew what a mistake that was the minute it happened. And not just because you walked in on us. That much I can promise you."

"Oh," I responded, absently.

After another short pause, Rip asked, "So, do you forgive me? For abandoning you?"

I couldn't help but smile as I gazed up into his pleading eyes.

"How could I not?" I smiled, even though part of me still wanted him to suffer, if only for a little while longer.

He then proceeded to take both my hands in his and pulled me up onto the couch with him.

I sat cradled in his arms for an indefinite amount of time, feeling truly content, and eventually I drifted off into a peaceful, satisfied sleep.

*****

"I'm leaving," Julienne declared as she stepped through my front door a few days later.

"What?" I was in shock.

"Not forever, honey. Relax," she laughed.

"Good," I said, relieved.

"I'll just be out of town for a few days. I'm playing drums for someone at a music festival." She sounded genuinely excited.

"When do you leave?"

"Right now," she announced with a smile. Typical Julienne. She didn't let anyone know what her plans were until the very last minute, because usually she herself didn't know what her plans would be until the very last minute.

I suddenly felt inexplicably sad. Even though Julienne would only be gone a short while, I'd still miss her constant company.

"Hey, buck up," she said with a grin, placing a comforting hand on my shoulder. It was as if she could sense how I was feeling. "I'll be back by Monday. Promise."

I gave her a weak smile in response.

"I'll bring you back a souvenir," she said as she closed the door behind her.

While Julienne was away, I did my best to keep myself busy. Whenever I was not occupied with my artistic duties, I would lie on my bed or the couch or even the floor, and simply watch the ceiling. Arbie called it lazing about. I called it 'lapsing into states of prolonged rest', or 'searching for inspiration.' Mostly I just lounged around thinking of nothing in particular.

On the night that Julienne was supposed to return, Rip came to visit me.

"Are you excited that she's coming home?" he asked from his usual spot on my couch.

"M-hmm," I answered, whilst rummaging in my fridge for something to feed him.

A knock at the door startled us both. Rip got up to answer.

Arbie strode into my living room, a grave frown imprinted on his forehead.

"What's wrong?" I asked immediately.

He hesitated a moment.

"Tell me," I insisted.

He sighed and led me to the couch, making me sit down. "What's going on?" Rip asked.

"There's been an accident," he began. I didn't need to hear any more. I could tell where this was going. Silent tears made their way freely down my cheeks.

"Julienne?" Rip didn't even need to ask. All Arbie could do was nod.

"She's at the hospital now, but they don't know if..." he trailed off.

I couldn't believe what I was hearing. I'd never lost anyone like this before. What would I do if she didn't make it? She kept me from all the bad things. Or she kept all the bad things from me.

With her around I never needed medication to perform on stage. She was a support system to me, albeit an unorthodox one. But she was more than that. She was one of my closest friends. If I hadn't met her when I had, I might have spiraled even further down into my own unhappiness. I would have allowed my insecurities over Rip and Isabella to consume me, but somehow, Julienne kept that from happening. She was the unconventional barrier between me and my bad habits. Without her, I would hit rock bottom harder than ever before. And I wasn't sure if I would be able to make it back up again, like I had before. That much I knew.

"I have to see her," I said, rising determinedly from the couch.

Rip and Arbie stood unmoving, staring at me in silence, neither of them sure what to do.

"Now," I practically shouted.

I was expecting them to keep me from going, but instead Rip grabbed his car keys from my coffee table and seized my hand. "Let's go."

*****

The hospital waiting room smelled of disinfectant and unfulfilled expectations. Arbie paced up and down the small room while Rip and I sat quietly in uncomfortable chairs, still trying to collect ourselves. By now I had given up trying to hold back my tears. I cried openly and without restraint until my face went numb and I felt empty inside.

The wait was agonizing. I jumped from my seat when a doctor approached us.

"Are you the family of Julienne Tracy?" she asked us.

"We're friends of hers," Arbie answered. "She doesn't have any direct relatives."

"I'm sorry," she began.

No.

I could feel my legs collapsing beneath me. I sank to my knees and tried to catch my breath.

No. No. No.

"There was nothing we could do," the doctor whispered. "I'm so sorry." Sensing that there was nothing she could do to remedy the situation, the doctor left us to absorb the news.

Rip crouched down next to me. His eyes glistened with tears.

He tried to pick me up from the floor, but I resisted. A series of dry sobs escaped my throat.

Rip and Arbie stared hopelessly at each other. I felt ashamed of my selfishness. Julienne had been their friend too, after all. I got up from the hospital floor and made an attempt to dry my eyes. I wondered where I would get the strength to carry myself through this.

Julienne's funeral was excruciating. I struggled – and often failed – to compose myself throughout it. Sometimes Rip would give my hand a slight squeeze, as if to remind me that he was still there. The entire ordeal was an incoherent, nightmarish blur. I remember crowds of faceless individuals offering me their condolences. I remember people I had never met before singing Julienne's praises. I remember feeling just about ready to break down as they lowered her into the ground. But that was all.

When I closed my front door behind me, the realization finally – and fully – struck me. She was gone. My friend was gone and I would never see her again. She was strong when I couldn't be. She helped me see things differently; she made me see the almost macabre bright side to just about every situation. And now she was gone.

In the weeks following the funeral, I isolated myself more and more from the world. I ignored all phone calls. I took no notice of knocks on my front door. I slipped further and further away from reality. I wanted to detach myself from everyone and everything. My whole life, I had felt like I was floating. Floating between friends, floating between states of mind, floating between groups of familiar strangers who never paid much mind to the fact that I was there. It was not that they abhorred my presence, or mildly disliked it even. It was more that they didn't notice it. But with Julienne around, that feeling of floating went away. She gave me a sense of stability that I hadn't been able to experience since the night of her accident. I tried to find that stability in my anxiety medication, but it only made me feel worse about myself. I felt guilty every time the phone rang. I knew it was either Arbie or Rip, doing their best to check on me, even though they themselves were trying to deal with their own pain. Their own loss. I felt like I was letting them down by sinking back into my old ways. I drowned my guilt in sleep and cheap wine. I tried to construct a temporary world for myself, where I could build a barricade against the hurt. But my little makeshift universe couldn't last forever. Soon before long, I knew I would be unraveling again.

I drifted off into a dreamless, rough sleep. I didn't even notice that Rip had let himself into my house. When I awoke, he sat at the foot of my bed. He seemed concerned, and rightly so, too, I supposed.

"I think you should stay with me for a few days," he said, softly.

This time, I didn't even bother to oppose him. I didn't have the strength.

I allowed the familiarity of Rip's house to envelop me. It was comforting and reassuring. Rip left for work the next morning, but only after I assured him over and over again that I would be fine on my own. I spent the majority of the day gazing down at the city streets from his bedroom window. I looked at the cars, whirring noisily by, like blurred brush strokes on a noisy canvas. I stared at the pedestrians on the sidewalk, each making their own way to nowhere in particular, none knowing where the other was off to as they brushed by each other. Some seemed almost comical in their haste; while others would, at times, come to a standstill in the pulsating crowd like a rock in a gushing stream. These were the ones I watched most intently. They had a certain mystery to them, a sense of secrecy I wished to unveil. Like the weeds blossoming from the pavement, reaching towards the sun, they wished to be more. Feel more. To rise above what was around them. To ascend from the muck and the grime that was their lives into something new. Something bigger than themselves. Something extraordinary that might give their lives a sense of meaning. Or so I liked to think, at least. I felt like that was what I would have thought if it were me standing on the sidewalk, letting strangers rush past me as I stared aimlessly into the polluted clouds. But instead I was trapped. Not in Rip's house, but rather within myself.

Rip finally felt comfortable enough to leave me alone during the day, and he was too tired to make much conversation when he came home at night. I kept reminding myself that this was weighing down on him, too.

One morning I gathered up all my courage and ventured out into the city. In the crowds on the streets, I could be what I was most good at in my younger years – anonymous. As long as nobody recognized me, of course. It was so easy to disappear when I wove myself into the masses. I had spent the majority of my life going unnoticed for the most part, until recently, anyway. I still somewhat prized my solitude. Standing in the streams of people, drowning out the noises around me, I realized that my isolation had become who I am. It had become a part of my being, fused into my soul. As this realization flooded over me, I saw a familiar face in the crowd. My logical mind told me it was impossible, and yet I went after her. Julienne disappeared around a corner, and I followed, only to discover that she was gone.

She was gone. Of course she was.

It was like experiencing her death all over again. I ran back to Rip's place and slammed the door behind me, gasping for air. It felt like the walls were closing in on me. Smothering me.

Rip looked surprised and slightly confused when he came home later that day to find me sitting in a pitiful heap on his kitchen floor, clutching a bottle of his best wine.

"What's the matter?" he asked, joining me on the floor and gently trying to pry the bottle from my hands. I didn't respond. Instead I began to sob pathetically.

"What's going on?" he asked again, his tone much harsher this time.

"I saw her," I managed to choke out.

His expression changed from confused to understanding in an instant. I didn't have to explain any further, he knew exactly what I meant.

"I think I see her all the time," he replied.

"You don't understand!" I snapped back, defensively. "I'm telling you, I saw her!"

He moved away from me, resting his back against the kitchen cabinets. He took the bottle with him. "Don't do this," he sighed, resting his forehead between his thumb and forefinger.

"Do what?" I demanded.

"Don't make this all about you!" He was shouting now. He took a swig from the bottle and continued, "She was my friend too. Or did you forget? Do you honestly think you're the only one who's affected by this? Are you really that self-centered?"

No. That wasn't true. Not in the least.

"Every day, I think about how you must be feeling. How you must be hurting. It haunts me," I said, fighting back another storm of tears.

"Then don't make this any harder for me. Please." Rip got up from the floor, leaving me alone with my thoughts.

Is that really what he thought of me? That I was self-centered? I realized soon enough that I had no right to be offended. It was true. I knew it was. I had put Rip and Arbie through hell, without even once taking their feelings into consideration. My focus had always been on my own pain, my own problems, my own past. It occurred to me that Arbie and Rip knew more about my problems than I did about theirs. Which, in turn, made me realize what a terrible friend I'd been. I didn't deserve to have such good, tolerant people in my life. And yet I took them for granted. I wanted to fix that. To fix myself.

*****

Some time after my little moment of enlightenment, I set off to visit Arbie. I decided I had to keep busy in order to forget about the turbulent few weeks I had been through. And what better way to do that than to immerse myself in my work? Arbie seemed hesitant at first, but after I explained to him that working was the best way for me to rise from the ashes, so to speak, he gave in.

Soon enough I was performing again. It was good to be back in my element – without the help of medication. I had moved back to my own house, and things appeared to be going well, for once. Despite all this, there was this lingering feeling of dread that seemed to be following me. No matter how hard I tried, I couldn't shake it. Some nights I would struggle to sleep, wandering aimlessly around the house or simply laying in bed, forcing my eyes shut, hoping that it would compel me to sleep. It didn't.

It was on one of these restless nights that I wandered out onto the balcony for the first time. I stared at the passing cars. I breathed in their sounds as they drove by. I submerged myself in the city. On the following restless night, I took it even further. I stepped up onto the wide railing of the balcony, first one foot, then the other. It was liberating. As I stood there, arms outstretched, my life hanging in the balance, I had never felt more free.

It wasn't until the third night – which just so happened to be New Year's Eve – that I considered jumping. For what reason this thought occurred to me, I didn't know. I let my toes dangle over the edge of the railing. A light breeze played with my hair. I looked down at the street. I imagined that falling must be a lot like flying. Before I could elaborate on this thought, however, the phone rang.

Shaken from my trance and very nearly losing my footing, I steadied myself with a startled gasp as the ringing yanked me back into reality.

I rushed to the phone and answered just in time.

"I hope I didn't wake you," Rip said in his soothing voice from the other end of the line.

"No, I couldn't sleep anyway," I assured him, still out of breath from my sprint to the phone.

"Happy New Year," he said.

"Happy New Year."

"Have you ever felt like you were trapped inside your own skin?" he asked, suddenly. His question caught me off guard, and it took me a second to collect myself.

I heaved a heavy sigh and answered, "All the time."

After a very philosophical conversation of nearly three hours, we finally hung up.

In those three hours, I had barely said a word. Rip felt like talking, and for once, I let him. I felt I owed him as much. He spoke about his hopes, his fears, and everything about life that bothered him. I listened patiently and intently, doing my best to be as supportive as possible. When our conversation was over, my urge to stand on the balcony's railing diminished somewhat. I felt lighter, as if I had somehow been able to help Rip simply by lending him my ears. It was my way of repaying him for putting up with me all those years.

The following day, however, my desire to jump was back. I couldn't place what had instigated this, but I knew that it was becoming harder and harder to stop myself. I awoke to a bright and clear morning. Vivid sunlight stretched across the room. Even though the morning was undoubtedly a lovely one, a mysterious and inexplicable sadness still crept over me. I stepped out onto the balcony once more. It, too, was bathed in sunshine. I started by leaning over the rail, taking in the sounds of the traffic below, as I had so many times before. The street beneath me looked so different in the daylight. Then, I climbed up onto the railing, as was my habit. It was just wide enough for my feet to rest comfortably on it. I extended my arms in order to keep my balance. My mind wandered back to my first hospital stay. I recalled Arbie's worried face. It was the first thing I saw when I woke up. He had taken such good care of me. More than I could ever have deserved. And then, of course, my second trip to the hospital. This time with Rip warding at my bedside as well. Perhaps if I went through with this, it would be better for them both, in the long run. They would have no hospital bed to watch. They would have no erratic friend to worry about. Somewhere in the depths of my subconscious the thought arose that maybe I was being selfish again. That maybe this would do both of them irreparable harm. This thought came to me a little too late, though, as I was already in the process of stepping off the balcony's railing.

*****

My stomach dropped and I prepared myself for the plunge.
But it never happened.
Someone seized the back of my shirt before I could fall. The shock momentarily clouded my vision and it took me a minute to register who my savior was. When the adrenaline finally stopped surging through me and my sight became clear, I looked up into Rip's eyes.

"This is by far the most idiotic thing you have ever done." He was furious. And crying. Unashamedly weeping. Even though he was livid, he held me anyway.

"I don't deserve you," I whispered.

"No. No you don't. But I'm here now, aren't I?"

We went inside. Rip sat me down on the bed and stayed with me until I fell asleep from sheer exhaustion.

When I awoke, I heard him having a heated telephone conversation. It didn't take me long to figure out that he was speaking to Arbie.

"Listen to me," he huffed, "I'm taking her to see someone – something which you should have done long ago."

There was a pause before Rip spoke again, "Then why didn't you, Arbie? You knew she needed help. You knew! But you couldn't afford to lose her, could you? Her success is your success, right?"

Another pause.

"We could have avoided all this," Rip sighed after a while. After he had hung up, he came back into my room. "You never did tell me why you ran away from home," he said as he sat down on the bed.

"I told you that you'd understand why after seeing the inside of my house," I answered.

"Yes, and all that told me was that your mother couldn't have been the greatest person to live with. There must have been another reason," he persisted.

"There was," I admitted.

"Then tell me. Please, tell me."

I sighed. "She hit me, okay?" I blurted out.

"Your mother?"

I nodded.

"Oh."

*****

"And that's about the time Rip brought you to me?" my therapist said, after taking in everything I had told her.

"Yes. He said it would be best for me. For both of us."

"How so?" she asked.

"He figured maybe this would keep me from doing something stupid again," I said, staring at my feet.

"Do you think so, too?" she enquired again.

"I do. Or at least I think I do," I answered after pondering it for a moment.

She wrote something on her notepad before looking back up at me.

"I'm going to ask you something, and I need you to be very honest. Can you do that for me?"

I nodded.

"Good," she said with a smile. Then her expression turned serious. "You appreciate having someone like Rip in your life, don't you?"

"Yes," I whispered.

She scribbled on her notepad again.

"Would you go as far as to say you love him?" she asked.

I hesitated before answering. "Yes."

"Then don't you think it's time you told him that?"

"I think it is."

I left the therapist's office feeling unusually happy. Elated, really. I hadn't felt so content in a very long time. I would go home, invite Rip over, tell him how I felt, and hope that he could forgive the way I'd treated him. I knew I wasn't worthy of his forgiveness. But I had to at least try.

I reached my house in high spirits and strode happily into the living room. As I walked in, something on the coffee table caught my eye. It was a single red rose, with a note:

I've decided it would be better for us both if I went away.

I know you aren't in a very good place right now, but to be honest, you never have been.

By the time you read this, I will be on my way to Spain.

I wish you nothing but happiness. Really, I do. But I can't do this anymore.

I'm so sorry.

- Ripley

THE END

www.ingramcontent.com/pod-product-compliance
Lightning Source LLC
Chambersburg PA
CBHW071219130626
46555CB00004B/1766